Sha...

Encouraging children to develop a l...
of books helps their literacy now and makes a difference
to their whole future.

One of the main ways you can do this is by reading
aloud. It's never too early to start – even small babies enjoy
being read to – and it's important to carry on, even when
children can read for themselves.

Choose a time that suits you both and a place
that's comfortable.

Don't worry about being good at reading.
Your voice is one of the sounds your child loves best.
Encourage them to join in with rhymes or repeated phrases,
and to tell you the story in their own words.

Take time to look at the pictures together.
Pictures help tell the story that's written, but often
tell their own stories too.

It's a good sign if children comment and ask questions as
you read. It shows they're interested. Talk about the book.
Was it good? Were there any favourite moments?

Read aloud as often as you can – new stories
and old favourites!

For Sophie
M.W.

For Felix
L.H.

First published 1997 by Walker Books Ltd
87 Vauxhall Walk, London SE11 5HJ

This edition published 2000

2 4 6 8 10 9 7 5 3 1

Text © 1997 Martin Waddell
Illustrations © 1997 Leo Hartas

The right of Martin Waddell to be identified as author of this
work has been asserted by him in accordance with the
Copyright, Designs and Patents Act 1988.

This book has been typeset in Galahad.

Printed in Hong Kong

British Library Cataloguing in Publication Data
A catalogue record for this book is
available from the British Library.

ISBN 0-7445-6818-8

Mimi Mouse's Christmas

Martin Waddell

Leo Hartas

WALKER BOOKS
AND SUBSIDIARIES
LONDON • BOSTON • SYDNEY

Mimi lived with her mouse sisters and brothers beneath the big tree.

"Santa Mouse will come soon," Mimi told her mouse sisters and brothers, as they huddled up close to the fire. "You must write your Santa Mouse notes, so he will know what to put in your stockings."

The mouse brothers and sisters started scribbling their Santa Mouse notes.

They scribbled ...

and they scribbled ...

and they scribbled ...

and they scribbled ...

and they scribbled.

"I can't write Santa's note by myself,
I'm too small!" Hugo told Mimi.
"I'll do it for you," said Mimi. "Tell me
what to write."
This is the note Mimi wrote.

"Does Santa Mouse have drums?" asked Hugo, when they were hanging the lights on their very own mouse Christmas tree.

"Well, he might have a small one," said Mimi. "It has to fit in your stocking."

"A small drum that makes a big BOOM when you bang it?" said Hugo.

"Just wait and see, Hugo," said Mimi.

Christmas Eve came and it snowed. The mice tumbled and jumbled about in the snow.

They tumbled ...

and they jumbled ...

and they tumbled …

and they jumbled …

till they all looked like little white mice!

"Supper!" called Mimi, and her mouse
sisters and brothers came in from the snow.
They had a Christmas Eve feast, huddled
close to the fire with mouse lemonade
and mouse cake.

"Let's leave Santa Mouse some,"
Mimi said, and she put mouse cake
and mouse lemonade out for Santa,
under the mouse Christmas tree
in her garden.

"Time for bed, sleepyhead!" Mimi said.
Hugo hung up his mouse stocking at the end
of his little mouse bed. It was a very big
stocking, though he was a very small mouse.
"Is it big enough for my drum?"
Hugo asked.
"Just wait and see, Hugo,"
said Mimi.

The mouse sisters and brothers dreamed of
the toys Santa Mouse would bring for their
mouse stockings.

They dreamed ...

and they dreamed ...

and they dreamed ...

and they dreamed ...

and they dreamed.

All of them dreamed except Hugo.
Hugo was such a small mouse that he felt
too excited to sleep. He got out of bed
and he looked, but there wasn't a drum
in his stocking.

Hugo went looking for Mimi.
"I can't get to sleep and that means
Santa Mouse won't come," Hugo told
Mimi, and he started to cry. "There
won't be a drum in my stocking!"

Mimi took Hugo out to the garden.
"Santa Mouse always comes," Mimi said.
"He comes when our mouse world's asleep.
That's how Santa Mouse works."

Mimi put Hugo to bed. And the next morning …

BOOM! BOOM! BOOM!
"Hugo's got his drum," Mimi's mouse sisters and brothers told Mimi. And …

Christmas was noisy at Mimi's!

Bear Hugs is a range of bright and lively picture books by some of today's very best authors and illustrators. Each book contains a page of friendly notes on reading and is perfect for parents and children to share.

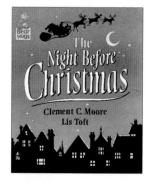

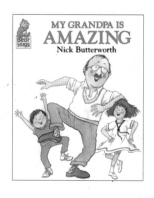

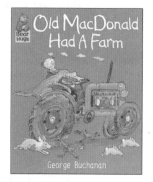

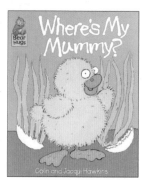

Cuddle up with a Bear Hug today!